到了金星請左轉

Hang a Left at Venus

丹·葛林寶（Dan Greenburg）著／陳家輝　譯
傑克·戴維斯（Jack E. Davis）繪圖

目次
Contents

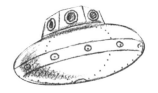

推薦序：聽得下去，才聽得進去　　劉經巖

聽得下去，才聽得進去

劉經巖◎撰

我有一個十歲的女兒和八歲的兒子，過去十幾年，因為工作上的需要與調動，我與家人曾經在不同國家、不同的城市居住過，兩個孩子不但在國外出生，也隨著我經歷了必須橫跨太平洋與大西洋，去找尋下一個家園的日子。這種因為遷就工作調動而經常與其他文化接觸的宿命，固然讓我與孩子得藉以觀察異國文化，增廣視野，這些經年累月的異國生活經驗與見聞，也讓我不得不更加重視在親子教育的努力。因為他們的世界比起一般的孩子更多彩多姿，他們的朋友、同學、玩伴甚至於學校的老師，除了美國人之外，可能是個俄羅斯人，也可能是個印度人；可能來自加拿大，也可能來自加勒比海地區。

我一直希望協助孩子在不同的國度中能怡然自得地面對他們所居處的環境，培養較恢弘的生活視野，同時培育他們兼具東方與西方世界之人文素養與合時宜的價值觀。但最重要的課題仍在於：如何讓他們在成長過程中瞭解到這個社會裡有真實殘酷的一面，但又不要失去對浪漫理想的追求。

　　因此，儘管工作再忙碌，我儘可能地撥空每晚在孩子入睡前，為他們說上一兩則「床邊故事」，我也花了很多時間跟精神尋找適合他們的床邊故事，從人物傳記、到寓言故事、童話勵志小品等，應有盡有。坊間的童書的確不乏佳作，但許多類似王子與公主從此過著幸福快樂的日子的故事，浪漫得不切實際；或有時講述到頭懸樑、錐刺股的勵志苦讀情節，在今天聽來，除了驚悚，也不太能引發孩子的共鳴，我當然也不會允許他們去效法的。

　　當哈佛人出版社張執行長將「札克檔案」初稿交給我時，我發覺這套書頗有些與眾不同，當我為孩子讀完「札克檔案」第一、二集的初稿，他們的反應是很興奮，而且不停地追問：還有沒有札克故事的續集？

　　兩個孩子的反

應讓我產生好奇，仔細分析後發現「札克檔案」是一套在真實生活時空環境下，充滿了想像力與各式新奇有趣事物的故事集，但這套書引人入勝之處在於，它的驚奇之處與我們生活細節環環相扣，故事鋪陳與發展的過程非常自然，而且故事情節常常出人意表，可謂「情理之中，意料之外」，足以引發孩子濃厚的興趣，因為他們不知道接下來會發生什麼事？因此，這些故事啟發他們的「好奇心」和「想像力」，使他們欲罷不能。

我也觀察到孩子們聽完故事後的反應——他們除了覺得札克的故事很有趣、很好笑之外，還因為他來自於單親家庭而有一點同情他。但我的詮釋是——在札克的世界中（他生長在美國紐約一個單親家庭，是個有點早熟而且EQ頗高的孩子），有大量的獨處時間，也才會發生這麼多稀奇古怪的事情。單親家庭已經是台灣與美國社會甚為普遍的一種家庭型態，我認為作者從單親家庭孩子眼中創造了一個充滿想像的世界，不僅不再讓單親家庭被賦予負面形象，讓這個現象不再象徵一種悲情或是一種禁忌。而或許這也為我們社會開啓了另一種思維方向，不再為單親家庭套上「不快樂的」刻板印象。

　　從家長的角度來看，我發現札克故事在字裡行間很忠實地介紹了美國社會裡真實的生活層面。像在《我的曾祖父是貓》裡就描述了美國小孩如何到動物收容所辦理領養寵物；又例如到銀行提款時一定要出具當事人證明身分和簽名等金融秩序。而故事中也常不著痕跡地帶出美國的價值觀，例如：莫瑞思曾祖父曾從事各種發明，而發明本身也是一種投資行為；最後他為臘腸狗設計專用的衣服終於為他賺進大筆財富。這些事例讓小孩子看到非常道地的美國精神，那就是一種拓荒冒險精神，勇於創新，鼓勵以創意與投資結合，造就名聲與財富，非常符合資本主義社會的生活基調。

　　在《藥櫃裡的神秘之旅》當中，提到美國孩子使用牙套的現象（也點出了小孩經常把牙套弄丟的生活插曲）、提到了札克要跟爸爸去參觀洋基隊的春季訓練營等等。這些對美國的孩子來說可是大事，而且是成長過程中不可缺少的大事！這些細微的情節都生動地描繪出小孩發育過程所面臨的一些尷尬以及棒球文化在美國、尤其在美國人父子關係間所具有的一種特殊地位。

所以，講述「札克檔案」的過程中，不但與孩子分享充滿想像力的故事，也介紹了美國的生活訊息，更教育了小孩生活中的各種面向。當然，對於曾在美國生活或是擁有大都市生活經驗的人而言，說這些故事是比較駕輕就熟的；但是對於沒有去過美國的人來說，這些故事也可以提供認識美國生活面向的題材。

這套書值得推薦的地方也在於——故事中有很多奇怪的構想，雖然會讓你覺得很神奇，但又不至於光怪陸離。這也回應本文最初我所提到的，為孩子挑選適合的讀物是許多父母共同的課題，「札克檔案」最為與眾不同的特色是，它以孩子的眼光看世界，幽默有趣、充滿想像空間；而我的

看法是——要讓小孩接受某個教育觀念，首先要讓他們笑、要讓他們開心，他們才會接受這些觀念，而不是嚴肅地說教或說些不切實際的故事。而「札克檔案」就是因為有趣，小孩子聽得下去，裡面所蘊藏的教育內容，他們也才聽得進去。

對那些「想要告訴孩子世界真實面貌，又不希望限制他們發揮想像力而不再嚮往新奇事物，怕孩子變得太世故」的父母親，如果您恰好在書店翻開這本書，何妨駐足瀏覽一番並試著向您的寶貝孩子講述這本書的內容，相信您與孩子都會有意想不到的收穫！

（本文作者目前任職於外交部，曾派駐美國華府、俄羅斯莫斯科等地服務，2004年為外交部選送至哈佛大學甘迺迪政府學院進修，並取得公共行政管理碩士學位。）

Chapter 1

I've always thought about being abducted by creatures from another planet. But when I finally came face-to-face with a real-life alien, I was the one doing the abducting! But I think I'm getting ahead of my story. First I should tell you who I am and stuff.

My name is Zack, and I'm ten and a half. I go to the Horace Hyde-White School for Boys. That's in New York. My parents are divorced, and I spend half my time with each of them. I was with my dad the night this UFO thing started.

平常我總幻想自己會被外星人綁架，但是終於和活生生的外星人接觸時，我反而成了綁架外星人的綁匪！喔，我大概一下子把故事說得太快了，應該先告訴你我是誰、並且介紹一些有的沒的才對。

我叫做札克，今年十歲半，就讀紐約市的赫瑞斯・海地懷特男校。我的老爸老媽離婚了，所以我輪流和他們住；而這個幽浮事件發生的那個晚上，我正好跟老爸在一起。

Dad and I had just left a movie in Central Park. I know it sounds weird, but sometimes they show movies at night in the park. It's sort of like a drive-in without the cars. And all around you are the twinkling lights of New York City skyscrapers. It's really cool.

Anyway, Dad and I were walking through the park to get a cab. Usually, walking through the park at night is a stupid thing to do. But there were lots of people from my school in the park. Plus, I was with my dad, so I wasn't afraid.

My dad is pretty brave. He's also very strong. He's a writer. I don't know if writing is what makes him strong. I do know he has

當時我和老爸剛看完電影，要離開中央公園。我知道這聽起來有點怪，但是中央公園晚上有時候會播放電影，有點像是戶外的汽車電影院，只是沒人開車來而已。在那兒看電影的時候，圍繞在四周的是紐約市摩天大樓一閃一閃的燈光，那種感覺真的很酷。

好啦，回到主題！那時我和老爸正穿過公園要去搭計程車。雖然通常只有笨蛋才會在晚上走在中央公園裡[註]，但今晚我有一大堆的同學也在這裡，加上老爸也在一塊兒，所以沒什麼好怕的。

我的老爸很勇敢，也很強壯。他是個作家，我不知道是不是寫作讓他變得強壯，但

註：紐約市的治安很不好，所以晚上走在中央公園裡易有人身安全的顧慮。

these very strong fingers from typing, though. He could squeeze your arm or your nose pretty hard if he wanted to.

We were walking up this path toward Fifth Avenue to get a cab. We passed by two people in trench coats. A man and a woman. They were holding flashlights and poking around in the bushes. The woman had reddish hair. The man had brown hair and a very worried expression. Dad and I shrugged and kept walking.

Then, just past this really tall hedge, I saw a weird glow.

"Hey, Dad," I said. "What's that weird glow up ahead?"

"Probably the light from one of the park

我可以確定的是，打字讓老爸的手指變得很強壯，他可以把你的手臂或鼻子捏得很痛。

我們朝第五大道的方向走去搭計程車，途中經過兩個穿著長風衣的人，他們是一男一女，手裡握著手電筒，往樹叢裡探頭探腦的；女人有一頭淡紅色的頭髮，男人的頭髮則是棕色的，一臉苦瓜相。我和老爸不以為意，繼續往前走。

接著，我們經過一排很高的樹籬，我看到一道怪異的閃光。

「嘿，老爸，」我說，「前方那道奇怪的閃光是什麼啊？」

「大概是公園路燈發出的光吧！」他

lampposts," he said.

"No," I said. "It's a different kind of light than that. It's an eerie glow."

"Well, we'll see what kind of glow it is when we get there," said Dad.

As soon as we got there, I saw what the glow was coming from. It wasn't coming from a lamppost. It was coming from a large silver something. It was shaped kind of like a Frisbee. Round, but with a dome in the middle. It was about the size of a Honda Civic. It was floating about three feet off the ground. And it was glowing. Eerily. There was a little rope ladder hanging off the edge of it.

說。

「不是啦！」我說，「那和路燈的光不一樣，是一道很詭異的光。」

「好吧，等我們到了那裡，就會知道那是什麼光了。」老爸說。

一到那裡，我立刻就明白這道光是從哪裡來的了。它不是路燈發出來的，而是來自一個巨大的銀色物體。這個物體的外形像飛盤，圓圓的，但中間有個圓頂；而物體的大小就跟一輛本田喜美車差不多。它漂浮在距離地面大概三呎^{（註）}左右的空中，發出詭異的光，還有一條繩梯垂掛在它的邊緣。

註：1呎約等於30.48公分，因此這個圓形物體距離地面約有90多公分。

"Dad," I whispered. "What the heck is *that*?"

Dad looked really surprised. He just stared at the glowing thing and shook his head.

"I don't know, Zack," he whispered.

"Is it a UFO?" I whispered.

"Uh, oh no, no," he whispered. "Nothing like that. I'm sure it's something much more

「老爸，」我小聲地說，「那是什麼鬼東西啊？」

老爸一副很驚訝的模樣，只是盯著這個發出閃光的東西搖著頭。

「我不知道，札克。」老爸小聲地說。

「是幽浮嗎？」我小聲地說。

「嗯，噢，不是、不是，」他小聲地說，「不是那種東西，我確定它是一種比

ordinary than that."

"Then what is it?"

"Well, just now it's hard to say," he whispered. "It may be a new kind of park vehicle. It's not a UFO, though."

"Then why are you whispering?"

"Uh, I usually whisper when I discover things that look like UFO's but aren't," he said.

Just then we heard a noise in the bushes. Next thing we knew, this kid came out of the bushes. At least I thought it was a kid. It was kid-sized. But when it caught sight of us, it let out a little scream. Then it fell over. I think it fainted.

"Yikes!" I whispered. "What the heck is

『那個』正常得多的東西。」

「要不然它是什麼呢？」

「嗯，現在很難判斷，」他小聲地說。「應該是一種新的遊園車，但不是幽浮。」

「那你為什麼要這麼小聲？」

「呃，當我發現看起來像幽浮、但實際上不是幽浮的東西時，我通常都會小聲地說話。」他說。

就在那個時候，我們聽到樹叢裡有聲音，接著一個小孩從樹叢裡走了出來——至少我認為它是一個小孩啦！因為它的體型跟小孩一樣。但是當它看到我們的時候，它發出小小的尖叫聲，就倒了下去。我想它是昏過去了。

「天啊！」我小聲地叫，「**那是什麼鬼**

that?"

"Uh, probably a child," said Dad. "A boy from your school who went to the movie."

We crept a little closer.

"A boy wearing a tin-foil suit?" I said.

"Possibly," said Dad.

We crept a little closer.

"A boy with no hair, no ears, and a weird nose?" I said.

"Possibly," said Dad.

"I don't know any boys at school who wear tin-foil suits," I said. "Or boys who have no hair, no ears, and weird noses."

"Maybe it's...a boy you don't know," said Dad.

東西啊？」

「呃，大概是一個小孩吧，」老爸說，「讀你們學校，來看電影的男生。」

我們躡手躡足地走近一點。

「一個穿著錫箔裝的男生？」我說。

「有可能啊！」老爸說。

我們又走近了點。

「一個沒有頭髮、也沒有耳朵，但有奇怪鼻子的男生？」我說。

「有可能。」老爸說。

「我不認識學校裡有哪個男生是穿錫箔裝的，」我說，「或是有哪個男生沒有頭髮、沒有耳朵，但卻有個奇怪的鼻子。」

「也許它是……一個你不認識的男生。」老爸說。

"I think it's a creature from another planet," I said.

"We don't have any reason to believe that," said Dad.

"What do you think's wrong with him?" I said. "Do you think he fainted?"

"Probably," said Dad. He reached out and took the creature's wrist.

"What are you doing?" I said. I thought he was pretty brave even to be touching it. I told you my dad was brave.

"I'm trying to see if he has a pulse," said Dad. "Oh, good. He's got one."

Dad held the creature's wrist and looked at his watch.

「我想它是外星人。」我說。

「我們沒有任何理由相信這樣的事情。」老爸說。

「他是怎麼了啊？」我說，「昏過去了嗎？」

「大概吧。」老爸說。他伸出手捏住這個外星人的手腕。

「你在幹嘛？」我說。我覺得老爸真是勇敢，居然敢摸它耶！我就說我老爸很勇敢的，沒錯吧。

「我摸看看他有沒有脈搏，」老爸說，「噢，太好了，他還有脈搏。」

老爸一邊捏著這個外星人的手腕，一邊看著錶。

"Normal pulse is about seventy-two," said Dad. "Your pulse goes up if you have a fever. Down if you're asleep or unconscious."

"What's this guy's pulse?" I asked.

"Three hundred forty-seven," said Dad.

"So that means...?" I said.

"Either he has a really high fever or he's a creature from another planet," said Dad.

「正常人的脈搏是每分鐘跳動七十二下，」老爸說，「發燒的話，脈搏就會變快；如果是睡著或昏迷，脈搏就會變慢。」

「那這個傢伙的脈搏是幾下？」我問。

「三百四十七下。」老爸說。

「那這樣是……？」我問。

「他如果不是發燒得很嚴重，就是個外星人。」老爸說。

Chapter 2

track-2

"So, Dad," I said. "At least you admit this is a creature from another planet."

"Or else a boy with a really high fever," said Dad.

"Have you ever heard of anybody who had a pulse of three hundred forty-seven?" I asked.

"Not really," said Dad. "Well, whatever he is, I think we have to revive him somehow."

"How about mouth-to-mouth?" I suggested.

"I don't think so," said Dad. "To tell you the truth, I'm not even sure which opening is the mouth."

第二章

　「這樣的話，老爸，」我說，「至少你承認這是個外星人囉！」

　「或是一個發燒得很嚴重的男孩。」老爸說。

　「你有聽過誰的脈搏是三百四十七下嗎？」我問。

　「是沒有啦，」老爸說，「不過不管他是什麼東西，我們得想個辦法讓他醒過來。」

　「要不要來個嘴對嘴人工呼吸？」我建議老爸。

　「我想不要比較好，」老爸說，「老實說，我甚至不確定哪一個開口是嘴巴。」

"How about giving him the old Heimlich maneuver?" I suggested. "You did that to me in that movie theater when I was choking on popcorn. Remember? You hug somebody from behind and squeeze."

"The Heimlich maneuver is used if you get a piece of steak or popcorn stuck in your throat," said Dad. "I didn't see him chewing steak or popcorn. Who knows what's wrong with him. I think we have to get him to a doctor, Zack. As soon as possible. I'll call Dr. Kropotkin from a pay phone."

Dad bent down and picked the creature up. We walked away from the UFO and headed toward Fifth Avenue. Dad found a pay

「還是幫他做哈姆立克急救法^{（註）}？」我建議，「就是那次我在電影院被爆米花噎到，你對我做的那一種。還記得嗎？從背後抱住，然後用力擠壓腹部。」

「只有在被牛排或爆米花噎住喉嚨的時候，哈姆立克急救法才派得上用場。」老爸說，「我沒看到他吃牛排或是爆米花，而且誰知道他是怎麼了？札克，我們應該帶他去看醫生，而且是越快越好。我要找個公共電話打給克波金醫生。」

老爸彎下腰把這個外星人抱了起來，我們離開這艘幽浮往第五大道走去。老爸找到

註：「哈姆立克急救法」是美國醫生Henry Heimlich於1974年發明的急救法，是用來急救因噎到而無法呼吸的人。

phone and called. Even though it was late, Dr. Kropotkin said to come straight to his home.

A cab stopped on Fifth Avenue. We got in. Dad lay the creature in the tin-foil suit down on the seat.

Dad gave the driver Dr. Kropotkin's home address.

The cab started forward. I could see the driver studying us in his rear-view mirror.

"What you got there, a sick kid?" the driver asked.

"Actually, we think it's a creature from outer space," I said.

"That right?" said the driver. "How about that. You know, I had a creature from outer space in my cab once."

一個公共電話並打了通電話；雖然時間很晚了，克波金醫生還是叫我們馬上去他家。

　　一台計程車在第五大道上停下來，我們坐了上去，老爸讓這個穿著錫箔裝的外星人在後座躺下。

　　老爸把克波金醫生家裡的地址告訴計程車司機。

　　計程車開始前進，我看到司機從後照鏡裡打量著我們。

　　「你們抱著的是什麼？一個生病的小孩嗎？」計程車司機問。

　　「事實上，我們認為它是個外星人。」我說。

　　「是嗎？」計程車司機說，「那我跟你說吧，我也曾經載過一個外星人。」

"Really?" I said. "Where did you take him?"

"Bloomingdale's," said the driver.

"What was he like?" Dad asked.

"He was a lousy tipper," said the driver.

"That's probably because he didn't understand our money," I said.

"I don't think that was it," said the driver. "I think he was just a lousy tipper."

When we pulled up at Dr. Kropotkin's, Dad gave the driver some money. Then we carefully pulled the creature out from the backseat.

「真的嗎？」我說，「你是在哪裡載到他的？」

「布魯明道百貨公司。」[註]計程車司機說。

「他長得什麼模樣？」老爸問。

「他是一個小費給得很少的乘客。」計程車司機說。

「大概是他不了解我們的幣值吧！」我說。

「我不這麼認為，」計程車司機說，「我想他只是一個小氣的乘客。」

我們在克波金醫生的家門口停下來後，老爸給了司機車錢，然後我們小心地把這個外星人從後座拉出來。

註：布魯明道百貨公司在美國是高檔的連鎖百貨公司，最初是在紐約市發跡，現在全美共有39家。

"You tip like you're from outer space," said the driver. Then he drove off.

Dad carried the creature into Dr. Kropotkin's apartment.

"Well, well, well," said Dr. Kropotkin. "Come in, folks. Zack, I haven't seen you in a while."

"No, sir," I said.

"The last time you were in my office, I believe you'd swallowed disappearing ink and were becoming invisible."

"That's right," I said.

"Well, it looks like you've recovered," he said.

"Yes," I said.

「你們給的小費就像外星人一樣少！」
計程車司機說完後就開走了。

　　老爸抱著這個外星人進到克波金醫生的
家裡。

　　「哎呀呀！」克波金醫生說著，「進來
吧，各位。札克，我有好一陣子沒看到你
了。」

　　「是啊。」我說。

　　「我想上次你來我診所的時候，你喝了
隱形墨水，變成隱形的。」^{（註）}

　　「沒錯。」我說。

　　「嗯，看起來你已經復原囉！」他說。

　　「是啊。」我說。

註：札克在第七集《你看得見我嗎？》裡不小心喝了好友史賓賽發明的隱形墨
　　水而變成隱形人。

"And how did I cure you?" said Dr. Kropotkin. "I don't recall."

"You didn't cure me," I said. "The heat from some TV lights I was standing under made me turn visible again."

"Ah," said Dr. Kropotkin. "So. Whom do we have here? A little friend from school?"

"Nope," I said. "A little friend from outer space."

"Ah. And what seems to be the matter with him?"

"He fainted when he saw us," said Dad.

"Well, let's have a look at him," said the doctor.

Dad carried the creature into the doctor's

「那我是怎麼治好你的呢？」克波金醫生說，「我記不得了。」

「不是你治好我的，」我說，「是電視台架的燈光產生的熱讓我現形的，當時我正好站在光的下面。」

「原來如此，」克波金醫生說，「那麼這是誰啊？你學校的小朋友嗎？」

「不是，」我說，「是一個從外太空來的小朋友。」

「喔，那他是怎麼了呢？」

「他一看到我們就昏倒了。」老爸說。

「嗯，我來看看他。」克波金醫生說。

老爸把這個外星人抱進克波金醫生的書

study. He put the creature down on a leather couch. The doctor shone a light in the creature's eyes. Then he looked in what seemed to be the creature's ear holes. And in what seemed to be the creature's nose. And in what we thought was the creature's mouth. Then the doctor took the creature's pulse.

房裡，將它放在一張皮沙發上。克波金醫生先用燈照著這個外星人的眼睛，之後對著像是耳朵的洞裡看，接著往看起來像鼻子的部位看，再來朝著我們覺得是嘴巴的部位看，最後量這個外星人的脈搏。

"I get three hundred forty-seven," said the doctor.

"And that's high, right?" I said.

"For a human, yes," said the doctor. "For a hummingbird, low."

The doctor put his stethoscope on the creature's chest and listened.

"How's his heart?" Dad asked.

"Fine," said the doctor. "Both of them."

The doctor wanted to give the creature a complete exam. We tried to take off the creature's tin-foil suit. There didn't seem to be

「我量到的脈搏是三百四十七下。」克波金醫生說。

「這樣的脈搏很高，對吧？」我說。

「對人類來說是很高，」克波金醫生說，「但對蜂鳥⁽註⁾來說是算低的。」

克波金醫生將聽診器放在這個外星人的胸口聽著。

「他的心臟還好吧？」老爸問。

「沒問題，」克波金醫生說，「兩個心臟都很好。」

克波金醫生想對這個外星人做更完整的檢查，於是我們試著脫掉這個外星人的錫箔裝，但那件衣服似乎沒有任何鈕釦或拉鍊；

註：蜂鳥是全世界最小的鳥類，只產於美洲。蜂鳥拍動翅膀的速度很快，每秒鐘可高達15至80次，速度之快除了可以盤旋在空中、維持姿勢吸食花蜜之外，還會倒著飛。此外翅膀發出的嗡嗡聲，也是英文名字hummingbird的由來。

any buttons or zippers. After a while we found a seam that just peeled open.

"Look at this," said Dad.

The creature was wearing a T-shirt with something written on it.

"What does it say?" asked the doctor.

Dad bent close to look at it.

"It's in some strange language I've never seen before," he said.

Just then the creature's eyes popped open.

過了不久，我們發現一個接縫脫了開來。

「你們看看這個。」老爸說。

這個外星人穿著一件T恤，上頭寫了一些東西。

「上頭寫了什麼？」克波金醫生問。

老爸彎腰更靠近地看著這件T恤。

「是一種我從來沒見過的文字。」他說。

就在這個時候，這個外星人的眼睛啪地睜開了。

Chapter 3

track-3

The creature screamed. Or what seemed to be a scream. It actually sounded a lot like yodeling. Then he tried to get up. Dad and Dr. Kropotkin held him down on the table.

"Calm down, little fellow," said Dr. Kropotkin. "We mean you no harm. We're just trying to help you."

"Can...you...understand...what...we...are... saying?" said Dad. Dad spoke very slowly and very loudly.

"Can...you...un-der-*stand*...what...we...are ...*say*-ing?" I repeated even louder.

第 三 章

　　這個外星人尖叫著——或者應該說像是在尖叫，而事實上聽起來更像是用假音在叫著。然後他試著要坐起來，但老爸與克波金醫生把他壓在桌上。

　　「冷靜點，小傢伙，」克波金醫生說，「我們無意傷害你，我們只是試著要幫你。」

　　「你…聽…得…懂…我…們…在…說…什…麼…嗎？」老爸說。他說得非常慢，而且非常大聲。

　　「你…聽…得…**懂**…我…們…在…**說**…什…麼…嗎？」我更大聲地重複說著。

"Please," said the creature in a high, metallic voice. "I may be from another planet—EEP—but I am not *deaf*."

"You speak English!" I said.

"Not precisely," said the creature. "I have—EEP—an omni-speak unit."

"Is that what's making those funny EEP-ing sounds?" I asked.

"Yes," said the creature.

"What the heck is an omni-speak unit?" said Dad.

"A small electronic chip in my mouth. It permits you—EEP—to hear what I say in any language you speak. It permits me to understand—EEP—what *you* say."

「拜託你們！」這個外星人以尖銳、金屬似的聲音說著，「或許我是來自別的星球──咿噗──但我沒有**耳聾**！」

「你會說英文耶！」我說。

「倒也不是，」這個外星人說，「我有一種──咿噗──萬用語言裝置。」

「是那種裝置讓你發出──咿噗──的好笑聲音嗎？」我問。

「是的。」這個外星人說。

「萬用語言裝置是什麼鬼東西啊？」老爸說。

「一種裝在我嘴巴裡面的小型電子晶片，它讓你──咿噗──以你說的語言來聽到我說的話，它也讓我可以聽懂──咿噗──**你們說的話。**」

"My name is Zack," I said. "This is Dad. And this is Dr. Kropotkin. What's *your* name?"

"BZ7943177568," said the creature. "But you can—EEP—call me BZ for short."

"This is amazing!" said Dad. "An actual creature from another planet! I didn't even know there was intelligent life on other planets!"

"Well, *I* did not know there was—EEP— intelligent life on *Earth*," said BZ.

"You didn't?" I said. "How could you not know that?"

"One cannot tell from deep space," said

「我叫做札克，」我說，「這是我老爸，這是克波金醫生。你叫什麼名字？」

「我叫『BZ7943177568』。」這個外星人說，「但你們——咿噗——叫我『BZ』就可以了。」

「太神奇了！」老爸說，「一個來自其他星球的真正外星人！我甚至不知道別的星球上有高等動物呢！」

「嗯，我也不知道地球上有——咿噗——高等動物。」BZ說。

「你不知道？」我說，「你怎麼會不知道呢？」

「一個來自宇宙深處的人是不會知道

BZ. "From deep space, Earth looks—EEP—like a dust bunny. And that is—EEP—on a *good* day."

"What does it say on your T-shirt?" Dad asked.

"It says—EEP—'My leader went to Earth and all he brought me was this lousy T-shirt.' It is a joke, Dad. People on my planet—EEP—do not believe there are T-shirts on Earth."

"Which planet are you from?" I asked.

"In your language—EEP—it would be called Fred."

"You're from the planet Fred?" I said. "Where's that?"

"You hang a left at Venus. You go into

的，」BZ說，「從宇宙深處來看，地球看起來就像是——咿噗——一團毛球，而且是在——咿噗——**晴朗**的天氣才看得到。」

「你的T恤上頭寫著什麼？」老爸問。

「它說——咿噗——『我的領袖去了地球，但他帶回來給我的只有這件髒髒的T恤。』這是一個笑話，老爸。在我們星球上的人——咿噗——不相信地球上有T恤。」

「你從哪個星球來的啊？」我問。

「以你們的語言來說——咿噗——它叫做『佛萊德』。」

「你來自佛萊德星？」我說，「那是在哪裡啊？」

「當你航行到金星的時候要左轉，就會

hyperspace—EEP—and get off at the first galaxy. We are the seventh planet on the right. You cannot miss it."

"If you didn't know there was intelligent life here," said Dad, "why did you come?"

"My fuel gauge is no longer working, Dad," said BZ. "My fuel was so low—EEP— I was forced to make an emergency landing. Imagine my surprise when I saw a city down here. What is it called, by the way?"

"New York," I said.

"New York?" said BZ. "That is—EEP—a

進入超空間^{（註）}——咿噗——接著在第一個銀河系轉進去，我們的星球就是右邊數來第七個，你絕對不會錯過它的。」

「如果你不知道這裡有高等動物，」老爸說，「為什麼還要來呢？」

「我的油錶壞了，老爸，」BZ說，「我的燃料只剩下一點點——咿噗——所以我被迫緊急降落，你能想像當我看到這個城市的時候，我有多驚訝嗎？對了，這個城市叫什麼名字啊？」

「紐約。」我說。

「紐約？」BZ說，「真是——咿噗——

註：「超空間」指的是比一般人能感受到的「三度空間」更高維度的空間，也稱為「高維空間」。高維空間理論認為在高維度空間裡，比較能夠看出自然法則的完整面貌；另外，在小說裡高維空間常被視作比光速更快的行進方式。

strange name."

"No stranger than calling a planet Fred," I said.

"Good point!" said BZ. "Intelligent— EEP—life on Earth! They are never going to believe this back on Fred. Ho ho!"

"You're low on fuel," I said. "What do you use for fuel in a UFO?"

BZ reached inside his tin-foil suit. He held up a small bottle of something.

"This is what we use," he said. "But my supply—EEP—is now exhausted. I do not suppose you have any of this on Earth, do you?"

He took the top off the bottle and handed it

奇怪的名字。」

「沒有比名叫佛萊德的星球來得奇怪。」我說。

「說得好！」BZ說，「地球上的——咿噗——高等動物！佛萊德星上的人絕對不會相信的。呵呵！」

「你的燃料快沒了？」我說，「幽浮是用什麼東西當作燃料的啊？」

BZ把手伸進錫箔裝裡，拿出一個不知道裝了什麼的小罐子。

「這就是我們的燃料，」他說，「但我的存量——咿噗——已經用完了。我想地球上應該沒有這種東西，你們有嗎？」

他把罐子上的蓋子打開，然後拿給我。

to me. I sniffed it.

"This stuff smells like mayonnaise," I said.

"Let me smell that," said Dad. I handed him the bottle. "Zack is right," he said. "It *does* smell like mayonnaise."

"Let *me* smell that," said Dr. Kropotkin.

Dad handed him the bottle. The doctor sniffed it. Then he dipped his finger in the bottle and licked it. The doctor was a brave man like Dad.

"Yep. It's mayonnaise, all right," said the doctor. "Hellman's Real Mayonnaise, in fact."

我聞了一下。

「這個東西聞起來像美乃滋。」我說。

「讓我聞聞看。」老爸說，我把罐子拿給他。「札克說得沒錯，」他說，「這聞起來**真的**像美乃滋。」

「讓**我**聞聞看。」克波金醫生說。

老爸把罐子拿給他。克波金醫生聞了聞，接著把手指伸進罐子裡，還舔了舔手指。克波金醫生真是跟老爸一樣大膽。

「是啊！這是美乃滋，沒錯，」克波金醫生說，「事實上，這就是黑梅牌正統美乃滋[註]。」

註：黑梅牌（Hellmann's）在美國是一家生產美乃滋的大品牌。1905年Richard Hellmann在紐約市開了一家熟食店，並且在店裡販售他太太調配的美乃滋醬，這就是美乃滋的問世。後來因為很受歡迎，因此也銷售到其他店面，甚至量產成為現在美國美乃滋產品的第一大品牌。

"We can go to the A&P and buy you enough to fly back to Planet Fred," I said.

"Then—EEP—I shall owe you my life," said BZ.

First we went to the A&P and bought eight jars of Hellman's Real Mayonnaise. The giant sized ones. Then we took off for Central Park and the UFO. It was a nice night, so we decided to walk. Lucky Dad is so strong because all those jars were kind of heavy.

When we got to Fifth Avenue, I saw something that gave me the creeps.

"Pssst, Dad," I said. "I think we're being followed."

「我們可以去A&P超市買一大堆，足夠讓你飛回佛萊德星。」我說。

「那麼──咿噗──我欠你一份大人情。」BZ說。

我們先到A&P超市，買了八大罐的黑梅牌正統美乃滋，而且是超大罐的那種；然後離開超市，前往中央公園裡幽浮停放的地點。當天晚上的天氣很好，所以我們決定散步走過去。幸好老爸非常強壯，因為那些罐子確實有點重。

但是當到達第五大道時，我看到某件事，讓我覺得毛毛的。

「嘶──老爸，」我說，「我覺得有人在跟蹤我們。」

"By whom?" said Dad.

I pointed.

"See that man and woman in the trench coats? They're the ones we saw in the park, poking around in the bushes."

Dad turned around. Then he turned back.

"They do look like the same people," he said. "But I don't think they're following us. They're probably just out for a stroll."

"Whatever you say," I said. Then I turned to BZ. "Do you have a long ride home tonight?"

"It is not too long," said BZ. "Only three thousand light-years. That is—EEP—a snap in hyperspace."

「誰在跟蹤我們？」老爸說。

我指給老爸看。

「你看到穿著長風衣的一男一女了嗎？他們就是我們在公園裡看到的那兩個人，當時他們在樹叢裡找東西。」

老爸轉身過去，然後又轉回來。

「他們看起來是同樣的人沒錯，」他說，「但我不認為他們是在跟蹤我們，他們也許只是出來四處晃晃而已。」

「隨便你怎麼說吧，」我說，然後轉向BZ，「你今天晚上飛回家要很久嗎？」

「不會很久，」BZ說，「大概只要三千光年^(註)就到了，在超空間裡——咿噗——只是一瞬間而已。」

註：光年是測量距離的單位，特別是拿來測量光在真空狀態中行進的距離。

"Still," said Dad, "we'd better get you back to your spaceship."

When we got back to Central Park we went right to the place where we'd left the spaceship. But it was gone! Vanished! Erased! Where the spaceship had been there was now only a burned ring in the grass.

「不管如何，」老爸說，「我們最好快

點帶你回到你的太空船。」

回到中央公園後，我們直接走向原本太

空船停放的地點。但是它不見了！消失了！

被移走了！之前停放太空船的地方，草地上

現在只剩下一個燒焦的圓圈痕跡。

Chapter 4

track-4

Poor BZ was really upset.

"Where is my spacecraft?" he kept saying over and over again. "What—EEP EEP— has happened to my spacecraft? It wasn't even mine. It was—EEP—a rental. And you know how unpleasant rental companies can be when—EEP—you lose their vehicles."

"While we were at the doctor's, somebody must have stolen it," Dad said.

"Has anything like this ever—EEP— happened before in New York?" asked BZ.

Dad and I looked at each other.

第四章

可憐的BZ非常地焦躁。

「我的太空船跑哪兒去了？」他一直反覆地說著，「我的太空船——咿噗咿噗——怎麼了？它甚至根本不是我的，而是——咿噗——租來的。你知道當你——咿噗——把太空船給弄丟了，太空船出租公司會有多生氣嗎？」

「一定是有人趁我們在醫生家的時候，把它偷走了。」老爸說。

「這種事——咿噗——以前在紐約發生過嗎？」BZ問。

老爸和我對看著。

"Every once in a while," I said.

"We'd better find a police station," said Dad.

"Freeze!" said a voice behind us.

We put down our plastic grocery bags, raised our hands, and slowly turned around. There were the man and woman who'd been following us. They both had guns pointed right at us.

「還滿常發生的。」我說。

「我們最好去警察局報案。」老爸說。

「不准動！」我們背後響起一個聲音。

我們放下塑膠購物袋，舉起雙手，慢慢地轉過身去。是那對跟蹤我們的男女，他們兩個拿槍指著我們。

"Wh-who are you?" I asked.

"I don't have to tell you. But I will. FBI," said the man. "I'm Special Agent Moldy. And this is Special Agent Scaley. Who are *you*?"

"My name is Zack," I said. "And this is my dad."

"And who is this?" said Moldy. He was pointing to BZ.

"A friend of ours," I said.

"We have reason to believe that one of you is an alien life-form," said Moldy.

「你們是、是誰啊？」我問。

「我沒必要跟你說，但我還是告訴你好了，我們是聯邦調查局的人。」男人說，「我是特別幹員穆迪，這位是特別幹員史凱莉⁽註⁾，**你們是誰？**」

「我叫做札克，」我說，「這是我老爸。」

「那他又是誰？」穆迪指著BZ說。

「他是我們的朋友。」我說。

「我們有理由相信，你們當中有一個是外星人。」穆迪說。

註：穆德（Mulder）與史凱莉（Scully）原是美國電視影集「X檔案」（X Files）中的男女主角，本書作者在此取了兩個諧音的名字。穆德是美國聯邦調查局（FBI）的探員，因為小時候目睹妹妹被人抓走，便懷疑是外星人犯下的，從此之後便深信所有不可思議的事情都有可能和外星人有關。史凱莉原本是一名醫生，加入聯邦調查局後被編入X檔案，負責監視穆迪；但與穆德經歷許多神秘的事件之後，反而開始信任他。X檔案在當年除了在劇中諷刺對政府的不信任之外，更表達了人們對於陰謀論、神秘事件與外星人的興趣。

"Assuming there *are* such things," said Scaley. "Which I personally doubt."

"Which one of you is the alien life-form?" said Moldy.

Nobody said anything.

"You might as well tell us," said Moldy. "We're going to find out anyway, sooner or later."

"I don't know what you're talking about," said Dad. "Nobody has ever proven there's intelligent life on other planets."

"See?" said Scaley to Moldy. "What have I been telling you?"

Moldy turned to BZ.

"What's your name, fella?" he asked.

「前提是真的**有**這種事情的話！」史凱莉說，「我個人是持懷疑的態度。」

「你們當中哪一個是外星人？」穆迪說。

沒有人出聲。

「你們最好主動招認，」穆迪說，「不管怎樣，我們遲早會查出來的。」

「我不知道你在說什麼，」老爸說，「還沒有人證明別的星球有高等動物。」

「你看吧，」史凱莉向穆迪說，「我不是一直這麼跟你說的嗎？」

穆迪轉向BZ。

「你叫什麼名字，小傢伙？」他問。

"His name is BZ," I said. "He goes to my school. The Horace Hyde-White School for Boys."

"Why don't you let *him* tell me?" said Moldy.

"Tell him, BZ," I said.

"My name—EEP—is BZ," said BZ. "I go to his school. The—EEP—Horace Hyde-White School for Boys."

"That's better," said Moldy. "But what's with the EEPs?"

"He has the hiccups," I said.

Suddenly Moldy pulled out his gun and stuck it in BZ's face.

"FREEZE OR I'LL SHOOT!" shouted

「他的名字叫做BZ，」我說，「他跟我上同一所學校——赫瑞斯‧海地懷特男校。」

「你為什麼不讓**他自己**跟我說？」穆迪說。

「BZ，告訴他。」我說。

「我的名字——咿噗——叫做BZ，」BZ說，「我跟他上同一所學校——咿噗——赫瑞斯‧海地懷特男校。」

「這樣才對嘛！」穆迪說，「但是那個——『咿噗』——是怎麼一回事？」

「他在打嗝。」我說。

突然間穆迪拔出他的槍，頂著BZ的臉。

「**不准動，否則我就開槍！**」穆迪大叫

Moldy.

Poor BZ fainted again.

"Hiccups gone?" asked Moldy in a friendly tone.

I revived BZ and helped him to his feet.

"I think so," I said.

"Never fails," said Moldy, putting his gun away. "Folks, we have reason to believe there was an alien spacecraft parked here earlier."

"Assuming there *are* such things," said Scaley. "Which I personally doubt."

"You people have any idea where this space vehicle might be now?" Moldy asked.

"Not at all," said Dad.

"I wish we did," I said.

著。

可憐的BZ又昏了過去。

「打嗝好了嗎？」穆迪用親切的語氣問。

我把BZ叫醒，扶他站起來。

「我想他好了。」我說。

「這招從來沒有失手過。」穆迪說著，並且把槍收起來，「各位，我們有理由相信，稍早之前有一架外星人的太空船停在這裡。」

「前提是真的**有**這種事情的話！」史凱莉說，「我個人是持懷疑的態度。」

「你們知不知道那艘太空船現在可能在哪裡？」穆迪問。

「我們完全沒有線索。」老爸說。

「我希望我們知道。」我說。

"Yeah?" said Moldy suspiciously. "Why do you wish that?"

"Uh, because we'd really like to see one," I said.

"Yeah," said Moldy. "Me, too. I'm afraid *They* got to it first."

"They?" I asked. "Who are *They*?"

Moldy looked around quickly.

"Let's just say I have reason to believe it's a government conspiracy," he said.

"Oh, Moldy, for crying out loud," said Scaley. "It's not a government conspiracy. You think *everything's* a government conspiracy."

"Everything *is*," said Moldy.

"Let's go, Moldy," said Scaley.

「是嗎？」穆迪懷疑地說，「你為什麼希望知道？」

「呃，因為我們真的想看看太空船長什麼模樣。」我說。

「是啊，」穆迪說，「我也想，但我怕**他們**捷足先登了。」

「他們？」我問，「**他們**是誰？」

穆迪快速地看了看四周。

「這樣說吧，我有理由相信這是一椿政府的陰謀。」

「噢，穆迪，你又來了！」史凱莉說，「這根本不是政府的陰謀。你總是認為**每件事**都是政府的陰謀。」

「每件事真的**都是**啊！」穆迪說。

「走吧，穆迪。」史凱莉說。

"I'd suggest you not tell anyone we had this little talk," said Moldy. He looked around to make sure nobody overheard us.

"Sorry to have troubled you, folks," said Scaley. "Say, do you need a lift home?"

"No, that's OK," I said.

"Nonsense," said Moldy. "We're not letting you walk through the park alone at night. *They* might abduct you."

"Our car's right over there," said Scaley. "C'mon."

Dad flashed me a worried look. We really needed to find BZ's spacecraft. But we couldn't do that till we got rid of Moldy and Scaley.

"A lift home would be great," said Dad.

「我建議你們不要把我們的對話洩漏給任何人知道。」穆迪說。他看了看四周，確認沒有人在偷聽我們講話。

「抱歉打擾你們了。」史凱莉說，「嘿，你們想搭便車回家嗎？」

「不用了，沒關係。」我說。

「這怎麼行？」穆迪說，「我們不會讓你們晚上獨自走在中央公園裡的，**他們**可能會綁架你們。」

「我們的車子就在那裡，」史凱莉說，「走吧。」

老爸向我露出擔心的神情。我們真的得找到BZ的太空船，但在沒擺脫穆迪和史凱莉之前，我們是沒辦法去找的。

「能搭便車回家真是太好了。」老爸說。

We picked up the mayo again and followed agents Moldy and Scaley.

As we walked, BZ leaned toward me and whispered, "You caused me to—EEP—tell an untruth, Zack."

"By saying you go to my school, you mean?"

"And by saying I am a boy."

"What?" I said.

"Zack," said BZ. "Can you not tell that I am—EEP—a Freddian girl?"

　　我們再次提起美乃滋，跟在穆迪與史凱莉探員後頭。

　　走著走著，BZ向我靠了過來，小聲地說：「你害我──咿噗──說謊，札克。」

　　「你是指你說我們上同一所學校嗎？」

　　「還有說我是男生。」

　　「那又怎麼了？」我說。

　　「札克，」BZ說，「你難道看不出來，我是──咿噗──佛萊德女孩嗎？」

Chapter 5

track-5

"Whoa!" I said. "You're a *girl*?" I could hardly believe my ears.

"And quite a beautiful one," said BZ. "On Planet Fred, all the boys—EEP—are always asking me for dates."

"Uh, cool," I said.

"Hey, guys," Dad called. "Walk a little faster, would you?"

We hurried to the car and got inside. Moldy and Scaley in the front. Dad, BZ, the mayo, and me in the back. Dad gave Moldy our address.

第五章

「什麼？」我說，「妳是**女孩**？」我真不敢相信我的耳朵。

「而且是個美女喲！」BZ說，「在佛萊德星，每個男生——咿噗——總是約我出去呢！」

「呃，那很棒啊！」我說。

「喂，你們兩個，」老爸叫著，「可以走快一點嗎？」

我們匆匆地走向車子，並且上車。穆迪與史凱莉坐在前座，老爸、BZ、美乃滋還有我坐在後座。老爸把我們家的地址告訴了穆迪。

I was still trying to get used to what BZ had told me when she whispered again in my ear, "Zack, do you think I am—EEP—beautiful?"

The last thing I wanted to do was hurt BZ's feelings. I wasn't too sure a girl with no hair, no ears, and a weird nose was beautiful. But I was willing to believe that back on Planet Fred she was a real babe. And people on Fred would probably think Gwyneth Paltrow was a real bow-wow.

"Uh, yeah," I said. "You're beautiful. Definitely."

"I think you are—EEP—beautiful, too," said BZ.

　　我還在試著接受BZ跟我說的那件事，這時她又一次在我耳邊小聲地說：「札克，你覺得我——咿噗——漂亮嗎？」

　　我很不想傷害BZ的感受，但是我不太確定，一個沒有頭髮沒有耳朵再配上一個怪鼻子的女孩，算不算是漂亮；但我願意相信，在佛萊德星上她一定是個漂亮寶貝，而且佛萊德星上的人大概會認為葛妮絲・派特羅^{（註）}是個醜八怪吧！

　　「呃，漂亮啊，」我說，「妳很漂亮，沒有人會懷疑的。」

　　「我也認為你——咿噗——很帥。」BZ說。

註：葛妮絲・派特羅（Gwyneth Paltrow）為美國著名女影星，曾以電影「莎翁情史」（Shakespeare in Love）獲得奧斯卡金像獎（Academy Award）最佳女主角獎。

"Thanks," I said.

Then she licked me on the hand. At least I *think* it was a lick. It was wet. It kind of creeped me out, if you want to know the truth. Maybe it was some kind of Freddian gesture of friendship. Like a slap on the back.

Moldy's cell phone rang.

"Agent Moldy," he said, answering. "Right. Really? No kidding. What's that location again? OK. We're on our way."

"What's going on?" Dad asked.

"An alien spacecraft has been spotted at the north end of the park," said Moldy. "We're going to investigate. I hope you folks don't mind tagging along."

札克檔案
到了金星請左轉

「謝謝！」我說。

然後她舔了舔我的手，至少我認為那算是舔，感覺溼溼的。老實說，這真的有點把我給嚇壞了。也許這是某種佛萊德式的友好表示，就像我們拍別人的背是一樣的。

穆迪的手機響了。

「我是穆迪幹員，」他回應著對方，「是。真的嗎？你不是在開玩笑？再說一次那個地點是哪裡？好，我們馬上到。」

「怎麼了？」老爸問。

「有人在公園的北邊發現一艘外星人的太空船，」穆迪說，「我們要過去調查一下，你們不介意跟著我們一道去吧？」

Dad, BZ, and I were very excited. We'd never have been able to find BZ's spacecraft on our own.

"We don't mind tagging along at all," said Dad.

"Neither do I," said BZ innocently. "I have always wanted to see—EEP—what an alien spacecraft looks like up close."

　　老爸、BZ還有我都很興奮，因為靠我
們自己是沒辦法找回BZ的太空船的。

　　「我們一點也不介意跟著你們。」老爸
說。

　　「我也是，」BZ裝無辜地說，「我一
直想要近距離地瞧瞧——咿噗——外星人的
太空船長的是什麼模樣。」

Chapter 6

track-6

In ten minutes we reached the north end of the park. Up ahead, just beyond the trees, we saw something. A weird glow in the sky. Searchlights.

"That must be it!" said Moldy excitedly. "This is an important moment for me, Scaley. I'm finally going to see my first UFO!"

He pulled the car to a stop beside some trees and parked. Moldy and Scaley took their guns out of their holsters.

"You people stay here," said Scaley.

"Right," said Dad.

第六章

十分鐘後，我們到達了公園的北邊。
就在前方樹林的後頭，我們看到了某樣東
西——一道來自空中的奇怪光線。那是探照
燈。

「一定是那個了！」穆迪興奮地說，
「這對我來說是個關鍵的時刻，史凱莉。我
終於要看到我生命中的第一艘幽浮了！」

他把車子開到樹林旁停下來。穆迪與史
凱莉從槍套裡拔出手槍。

「你們待在這裡。」史凱莉說。

「好的。」老爸說。

But as soon as Moldy and Scaley walked through the trees, we followed. BZ grabbed my hand in the darkness. She had quite a grip.

"BZ," I said. "I'm going to need that hand back."

"Why?" she said.

"Because any minute now, I'm going to have to scratch my nose."

"Scratch—EEP—with your other hand," she said.

As we followed Moldy and Scaley toward the weird searchlight glow, we noticed something else up ahead. A metallic Frisbee-shaped thing hovering over the trees. A UFO? BZ and I walked faster. Then, just ahead of us,

　　但是當穆迪與史凱莉一走進樹林，我們就跟在他們後頭。BZ在黑暗中抓住我的手，而且抓得很緊。

　　「BZ，」我說，「妳可以把我的手放開嗎？」

　　「為什麼？」她問。

　　「因為我需要那隻手來抓鼻子。」

　　「用──咿噗──你的另外一隻手抓啊。」她說。

　　當我們跟著穆迪和史凱莉往這道詭異的探照燈光前進時，我們發現前方還有某樣東西。一個金屬飛盤狀的物體在樹上盤旋。是幽浮嗎？BZ和我走得更快了。然後就在

Moldy and Scaley burst out of the trees and into a big clearing, guns out. We followed.

What we saw was a carnival. A Ferris wheel. A merry-go-round. A roller coaster, with cars in the shape of rockets. A stand that sold cotton candy. And there, on top of a giant crane, was a UFO.

Well, maybe not a real UFO. And certainly not BZ's UFO. It was a round, Frisbee-shaped, cheesy-looking thing that looked a little like BZ's. But not much. It had a big sign on it: GENUINE UFO FROM OUTER SPACE! NOT A FAKE! THIS IS THE REAL DEAL! ADULTS RIDE $1.00, KIDS 50¢! YOU MUST BE AT LEAST AS TALL AS THIS SIGN TO

我們的前方，穆迪與史凱莉衝出樹林，來到一個很大的空地，把槍舉起來。我們繼續跟著。

在我們眼前的是一個遊樂場，裡頭有摩天輪、旋轉木馬、火箭造型座椅的雲霄飛車和一個賣棉花糖的攤販，還有一台巨大的吊車吊著一艘幽浮。

好吧，應該說它不是一艘真正的幽浮，更絕對不是BZ的幽浮，而是一個圓形、飛盤狀、造型很遜的東西，看起來是有點像BZ的幽浮，但只有一點點像而已。上面有一個很大的招牌寫著：**來自外太空的真正幽浮！如假包換！超便宜！大人一次一塊！小孩一次五十分！**（註）**想操控這艘太空船的人**

註：這裡指的是美金，1美元大約等於台幣33元；另外100分（cent）等於一美元，所以50分約等於台幣15元。

COMMAND THIS ALIEN SPACECRAFT!

Moldy and Scaley just stood there. Guns out. Looking stupid. People were staring nervously at them. Finally Scaley put her gun away.

"I have never been so embarrassed in my entire life," she said.

"Yes, you have," said Moldy, putting his

至少得和這個招牌一樣高才行！

穆迪與史凱莉呆站在那裡，亮著槍，露出一副蠢相。大家緊張地看著他們兩個，最後史凱莉把槍收了起來。

「我這輩子從來沒有這麼丟臉過。」她說。

「有，妳有過，」穆迪說著，把槍放下

"Oh, right," said Scaley.

We walked back to where we'd parked the car. But the car was gone.

"Oh, poop!" said Scaley. She kicked the dirt.

"What happened to your car?" I asked.

"Stolen, obviously," said Scaley. She turned to Moldy. "Will you at least admit to me there's no such thing as a UFO?" she asked.

"Here's what I believe," said Moldy. "I believe *They* heard we were coming. I believe *They* replaced the real UFO with the fake one we saw. *They* were following us, and as soon as we got out of the car, *They* stole it. It's a

來，「就在昨天啊，記得嗎？」

「啊，對喔！」史凱莉說。

我們走回原本停車的地方，但是車子不見了。

「噢，天殺的！」史凱莉說，她用力踢著泥土。

「你們的車呢？」我問。

「用膝蓋想也知道，它被偷走了。」史凱莉說。她轉向穆迪，「你可以好歹承認沒有幽浮這回事嗎？」她問。

「妳知道我真正的想法嗎？」穆迪說，「我相信**他們**聽到我們要來，**他們**就把真正的幽浮換成我們看到的假幽浮。**他們**在跟蹤我們，當我們一下車後，**他們**就把它偷走

conspiracy, Scaley. Just as I've always thought."

Scaley slapped her forehead.

"Moldy, you are absolutely bonkers!" shrieked Scaley. "You are absolutely out of your mind! There is no conspiracy! There are no alien spacecraft! There are no little green men from outer space!" She turned to us. "Am I right, or am I wrong?"

"Well," I said. "I've never seen any little green *men*."

"See?" said Scaley. "Even this ten-year-old *kid* has more sense than you do!"

了。史凱莉，這是一樁陰謀，就跟我一直以
來所想的一樣。」

史凱莉打了一下自己的額頭。

「穆迪，你真的是個瘋子！」史凱莉
尖叫著，「你真的是發瘋了！這裡沒有任何
陰謀！這裡根本沒有外星人的太空船！這裡
沒有來自外太空的小綠人！」她轉向我們，
「不是嗎？我說錯了嗎？」

「嗯，」我說，「我從來沒看過任何小
綠『人』。」

「你看吧？」史凱莉說，「連這個十歲
的小孩都比你正常！」

Chapter 7

Moldy and Scaley stomped off into the dark, looking for their car and yelling at each other.

"I am very upset—EEP—that my spaceship is gone," said BZ. "There will be—EEP— terrible late charges from the rental company."

"We're going to find it for you, BZ," I said.

I don't know why I said that. I didn't have a clue where BZ's spaceship was. I just wanted to make her feel better.

I remembered there's a police station

第七章

穆迪和史凱莉重重地踏步走進黑暗中，一邊找著車子一邊互相叫罵。

「我很不安——咿噗——我的太空船不見了，」BZ說，「太空船出租公司會向我收——咿噗——嚇死人的延遲費用。」

「我們會幫妳找到的，BZ。」我說。

我不知道我為什麼要那麼說，因為對於BZ的太空船下落，我其實一點線索也沒有。我只是不想讓她這麼難過而已。

我記得中央公園裡有一個警察局，他們

in Central Park. They always help out with missing vehicles...although usually ones manufactured on this planet. With me leading the way, Dad, BZ and I walked to the Central Park Precinct. We marched right up to the sergeant behind the desk.

"Officer, we'd like to report a stolen vehicle," said Dad.

"OK," said the desk sergeant. He started filling out a form. "What was the make and year of the vehicle?"

I could see we were heading for trouble.

"I don't know," said my Dad.

"You don't know?" said the desk sergeant.

"No," said Dad.

總是幫忙人們尋找遺失的車輛⋯⋯不過通常

都是地球出產的那一種啦！我帶著路，老爸

和BZ跟著我走到中央公園警局，我們直接

走向值班警官。

「警官，我們要通報一輛失竊的車

輛。」老爸說。

「好的，」值班警官說著，他開始填寫

表格，「車子是什麼廠牌，幾年份的？」

看得出來我們正在自找麻煩。

「我不知道。」老爸說。

「你不知道？」值班警官說。

「我不知道。」老爸說。

I pulled on Dad's arm. "Uh, maybe we should leave."

"How could you not know?" said the desk sergeant. "Doesn't the vehicle belong to you?"

"Not me," said Dad. He pointed to BZ. "Him."

"Him?" said the desk sergeant. "He looks a little young to drive. How old are you, son?"

"Seventy-one parludes," said BZ.

"Excuse me?" said the desk sergeant, and he gave BZ a puzzled look. Then he said in a tired voice, "Just give me your license and registration."

"My what?" said BZ.

"He, uh, may not have the kind of license

　　我拉拉老爸的手臂說，「嗯，也許我們還是走吧。」

　　「你怎麼會不知道？」值班警官說，「這輛車不是你的嗎？」

　　「不是我的，」老爸指著BZ說，「是他的。」

　　「他？」值班警官說，「他看起來年紀有點小，不能開車喔，小朋友，你幾歲？」

　　「法定年齡七十一歲。」BZ說。

　　「什麼？」值班警官說，還狐疑地看著BZ。接著他以疲憊的語氣說，「給我你的駕照和行照。」

　　「我的什麼？」BZ說。

　　「他，嗯，可能沒有你想的那種駕照和

and registration you'd recognize," said Dad.

"He's from out of state?" said the desk sergeant.

"Yes, sir," said Dad. "*Way* out of state."

The desk sergeant stuck out his hand. "Papers, please."

BZ seemed confused. But she reached into her tin-foil suit and brought out a little rolled-up something. She unrolled it. It was a clear plastic sheet. Like Saran Wrap, only heavier. It had lots of writing on it. It looked like the writing on her T-shirt. She handed it to the desk sergeant.

The desk sergeant squinted at the clear plastic sheet. "OK, show me where it says the make and year of the car."

行照。」老爸說。

「他是從別州來的嗎？」值班警官說。

「是的，警官，」老爸說，「從**很遠很遠**的州來的。」

值班警官伸出手來，「證照拿來，謝謝。」

BZ看起來很困惑，但是她把手伸進錫箔裝裡，拿出一小捲東西。她打開它，那是一張透明的塑膠片，看起來很像保鮮膜^{（註）}，只是比較厚；上面寫了很多東西，就像她T恤上的文字一樣，她把塑膠片拿給值班警官。

值班警官斜眼看著這張透明塑膠片，「好吧，告訴我這車子的廠牌及年份寫在哪裡。」

註：保鮮膜是由saran這種塑膠原料所製成，在美國就有廠商拿saran這個字當做保鮮膜品牌。

"It wasn't exactly a car," said my dad.

"What was it, a motorcycle?"

"Not exactly," said Dad.

"Then what was it?"

"It was a more a...a spacecraft," I said. I really thought it was a mistake being here. But then the desk sergeant said, "A spacecraft? Wait a minute. Was that the round thing parked just off the Sheep Meadow, behind the trees?"

"You mean you saw it?" I said excitedly.

"We saw it, all right," said the desk sergeant. "It was illegally parked. We had it towed."

「它其實不算是一輛車。」老爸說。

「那是什麼，摩托車？」

「也不算是。」老爸說

「要不然是什麼？」

「它比較像是一艘⋯⋯一艘太空船。」
我說。我真的認為來這裡是個錯誤，但是
這個值班警官接著說，「一艘太空船？等一
下，是不是一台圓形的東西，停在綿羊草地
（註）邊的樹林後面？」

「你是說你有看到它？」我興奮地說。

「沒錯，我們是有看到它，」值班警
官說，「你們違規停車，所以我們把它拖走
了。」

註：中央公園的Sheep Meadow曾經是牧羊的短草地區，現在已成為紐約最受
　　歡迎的日光浴場。

"Towed?" I said. "Towed where?"

"Where we tow all illegally parked vehicles in New York," said the desk sergeant. "Pier 76. On Thirty-eighth Street and the Hudson River." He handed back the clear plastic sheet. "I suggest you go down there and pick it up as soon as possible. And it's going to cost you a bundle."

「拖走了？」我說，「拖到哪裡去了？」

「所有紐約市裡違規停車的車子都是被拖到七十六號碼頭，」值班警官說，「就在三十八街與哈德森河的交界處，」他遞回透明的塑膠片，「我建議你們盡快去取車，而且你們會被罰上一大筆錢。」

Chapter 8

track-8

The Department of Motor Vehicles clerk at Pier 76 had a beard and wore a beanie. Right away he started filling out a long Department of Transportation form.

"I want my spaceship back," said BZ.

"Sshhhh," I said.

"License and registration," said the clerk without looking up.

"BZ, give him your license and registration," Dad said.

BZ unrolled her sheet of plastic. The clerk

第八章

七十六號碼頭監理處的辦事人員留著鬍子，還戴著一頂帽子。他馬上動手填寫一份超長的交通部表格。

「我要拿回我的太空船。」BZ說。

「噓──」我說。

「駕照和行照拿來。」辦事員說著，完全沒有抬頭看我們。

「BZ，把你的駕照和行照給他。」老爸說。

BZ打開她的塑膠片，辦事員拿著它詳

took it and studied it closely. Then he began copying the strange symbols from BZ's roll of plastic onto his form. I guess he had seen other crazy registrations before. After a long time of filling out the form, he looked up again.

"One hundred seventy-five dollars, please," he said. "No checks or credit cards."

"Wow," said Dad.

"What—EEP—does he say?" asked BZ.

"He says the fine for parking is a hundred and seventy-five dollars," said Dad.

"Is that—EEP—much money?" asked BZ.

"Yeah," I said.

"BZ," said Dad. "You wouldn't happen to have any money, would you?"

細地看著，然後開始把塑膠片上的奇怪符號抄在他的表格上；我猜他以前也看過其他怪異的行照吧。他花了好長一段時間填完表格後，抬起頭來看著我們。

「一百七十五塊，謝謝，」他說，「我們不收支票或是信用卡。」

「哇塞！」老爸說。

「他——咿噗——說什麼？」BZ問。

「他說違規停車的罰金是一百七十五塊。」老爸說。

「這樣是——咿噗——很多錢嗎？」BZ問。

「是啊。」我說。

「BZ，」老爸說，「你身上不會剛好有帶錢吧，有嗎？」

"Oh—EEP—certainly," said BZ. "I always carry money."

"Thank heavens," said Dad.

BZ reached into her tin-foil suit and plunked something down on the counter. It was a diamond about the size of a bubble gum ball.

"I cannot make change for this," said the clerk. "Do you have anything smaller?"

"I am sorry," said BZ.

Dad took some bills out of his pocket and counted them.

"I've got exactly a hundred and seventy-one dollars," Dad said. "That's four dollars short."

"They won't give back BZ's spacecraft

「噢——咿噗——當然有啊！」BZ說，「我總是有帶錢在身上。」

「謝天謝地！」老爸說。

BZ把手伸進錫箔衣裡，拿出某樣東西重重地放在櫃檯上，那是一顆和泡泡糖差不多大的鑽石。

「我沒辦法找零，」辦事員說，「你有小一點的嗎？」

「抱歉，沒有。」BZ說。

老爸從他的口袋裡拿出一些鈔票數了數。

「我只有一百七十一塊，」老爸說，「還少四塊錢。」

「除非我們付清罰款，否則他們是不會

unless the fine is paid," I said.

"And they don't take checks or credit cards," said Dad. "What do we do now?"

I dumped out my pockets. In one I had a piece of Dubble-Bubble and an unwrapped sticky cough drop. In another I had two crumpled-up dollar bills and a bunch of coins. I counted out the coins. I had more than two dollars in change.

"I have four dollars and thirteen cents," I said. "With what Dad has, we've got the fine, plus an extra thirteen cents."

"Great," said Dad.

把BZ的太空船還給我們的。」我說。

「而且他們不收支票或是信用卡，」老爸說，「我們現在該怎麼辦呢？」

我把口袋裡的東西全部倒了出來，其中一個口袋裡有一片口香糖[註]和一顆沒用包裝紙包著、變得黏答答的喉糖。另一個口袋裡，有兩張皺皺的一元紙鈔與一堆銅板。我數了數銅板，總共超過兩元。

「我有四塊又十三分，」我說，「再加上老爸的，我們有足夠錢繳罰金，而且還多出十三分喔！」

「好極了！」老爸說。

註：美國費城的一名叫沃爾特‧戴默（Walter E. Diemer）的會計在1928年發明了泡泡糖，當時他把它叫做Dubble Bubble。但一直要到1937年，第一批泡泡糖產品才正式在全美上市。如今，泡泡糖產品雖然推陳出新，但大家依然稱作Dubble Bubble。

Dad handed the clerk his hundred and seventy-one dollars. I gave the clerk my four dollars.

Then BZ gave Dad her diamond.

"BZ," said Dad. "I can't take this."

"It is—EEP—not necessary to make change," said BZ. "You have been very kind to me. Please, keep the change."

老爸給了辦事員他的一百七十一塊，而我給了辦事員我的四塊錢。

接著BZ把她的鑽石給老爸。

「BZ，」老爸說，「我不能收下。」

「你——咿噗——不用找錢，」BZ說，「你們對我太好了，請把該找我的錢留著。」

"But this diamond is worth thousands of dollars," said Dad. "I couldn't possibly take it from you."

"Unless you take it, I shall—EEP—be very insulted," said BZ.

"Well," said Dad, "only if you're sure."

"I am sure," said BZ.

The clerk marked the fine paid. Then a man in blue coveralls led us back to the outdoor parking lot and showed us where they'd put BZ's spacecraft. The spacecraft wasn't glowing anymore. And it wasn't floating three feet off the ground.

"Aha!" said a voice behind us. "I thought

「但這顆鑽石價值好幾千塊，」老爸說，「我絕對不能拿你這顆鑽石。」

「除非你收起來，否則我會——咿噗——覺得受到羞辱。」BZ說。

「好吧，」老爸說，「如果你確定要這麼做的話。」

「我確定。」BZ說。

辦事員登記我們付了罰金，接著一個穿著藍色工作服的男人帶我們回到戶外停車場，告訴我們BZ的太空船放在哪裡。太空船沒有在發光，也沒有飄浮在離地面三呎的空中。

「啊哈！」我們背後響起一個聲音，

you said you didn't know anything about alien spacecraft."

We turned around. Agents Moldy and Scaley were standing right behind us.

"Hey," I said. "What are you doing here?"

Moldy and Scaley looked a little embarrassed. "Actually," said Moldy, "it turned out that *They* didn't steal our car after all. It was towed. But don't change the subject. Whose alien spacecraft is this?"

"This isn't an alien spacecraft," I said. "It's BZ's car. It's a rental."

"See?" said Scaley to Moldy.

"I've never seen a car like *that* before,"

「我想你們說過，你們完全不知道太空船的事。」

我們轉過身去，穆迪和史凱莉探員正站在我們的後面。

「嘿！」我說，「你們在這裡幹嘛？」

穆迪與史凱莉看起來有點不好意思。「事實上，」穆迪說，「**他們**沒有偷走我們的車子，車子是被拖走了。但是你不要改變話題，這艘外星人的太空船是誰的？」

「這不是外星人的太空船，」我說，「這是BZ的車子，是租來的。」

「你看吧？」史凱莉對穆迪說。

「我以前從來沒看過**這種**車。」穆迪

said Moldy.

"It's a foreign job," said Dad.

"Oh, I see," said Moldy. He seemed disappointed. "You *sure* it's not an alien spacecraft?"

"Pretty sure," said Dad.

"Oh, Moldy, for crying out loud," said Scaley. "It's not an alien spacecraft, OK?"

"And what makes you so sure?" asked Moldy.

"I happen to be a doctor, OK?" said Scaley.

"Right," said Moldy. "OK then. By the way, what kind of mileage do you get on this baby?" he asked BZ.

"What does he ask about babies?" said BZ.

說。

「這是外國車。」老爸說。

「喔，原來如此，」穆迪說，他看起來很失望的樣子，「你**確定**它不是外星人的太空船？」

「非常確定。」老爸說。

「噢！穆迪，你又來了！」史凱莉說，「這不是外星人的太空船，好嗎？」

「妳怎麼能如此確定？」穆迪問。

「我正好是個醫生，這樣回答你滿意嗎？」史凱莉說。

「好吧，」穆迪說，「那順便問一下，你這台寶貝的行駛哩數（註）是多少呢？」他問BZ。

「他在問什麼寶貝啊？」BZ說。

註：行駛哩數指的是車子每單位燃料可以跑的距離。

"He wants to know how far you can go on a gallon of fuel," I said.

"About—EEP—two thousand light-years per gallon," said BZ.

"Is that city driving, or highway?" asked Moldy.

"Highway," I said.

"What do you use, regular gas or premium?" asked Moldy.

"Mayonnaise," said BZ before I could stop her.

"Mayonnaise?" said Moldy. He was frowning. "You know, now that you mention it, there are eight jumbo jars of Hellman's Real Mayonnaise in the backseat of my car. They

「他想要知道你一加侖^(註)的燃料可以跑多遠？」我說。

「大概——咿噗——每加侖跑兩千光年。」BZ說。

「是在市區還是高速公路上行駛？」穆迪問。

「高速公路。」我說。

「你用什麼油？一般汽油還是高級汽油？」穆迪問。

「我用美乃滋。」在我來不及阻止之前，BZ這麼回答。

「美乃滋？」穆迪說，他皺著眉頭，「說到美乃滋倒是提醒了我，在我車子的後座有八大罐黑梅牌正統美乃滋，那不會剛好

註：1加侖約等於3.785公升。

wouldn't happen to be yours, would they?"

"Actually, they are," I told him. I'd forgotten all about them.

"Oh good," said Moldy, his frown gone. "That's another case solved! I thought maybe it was a case of psychic teleportation."

We got the mayonnaise out of the car, then agents Moldy and Scaley said goodbye. Moldy put one hand on my shoulder and one on BZ's. "Remember, kids," he said in a serious voice, "the truth is out there."

"Of course—EEP—it is," BZ said.

是你的吧，是嗎？」

「事實上，是他的沒錯。」我告訴他。
我完全忘記這回事了！

「太好了！」穆迪說，不再皺著眉頭，
「又解決一個案子了！我原本以為這可能是
心靈傳送器之類的。」

我們把美乃滋從車上拿下來，然後穆迪
和史凱莉探員跟我們說再見。穆迪把一隻手
放在我的肩膀上，另一隻手則放在BZ的肩
上，「孩子們，要記得，」他用認真的口氣
說，「真相就在那裡。」^{（註）}

「當然——咿噗——真相就在那裡。」
BZ說。

註：X檔案裡最經典的名句就是The Truth Is Out There.（真相就在那裡），其
　　他的還有：Trust No One. 和 I Want to Believe.

Moldy and Scaley got in their car, arguing the whole time. And that was the last I saw of them. Sometimes I wonder if Moldy ever did find proof of alien life.

"It is time for me to return to my planet," said BZ. "May I give you—EEP—a ride to your home?"

"Seeing as how we have only thirteen cents left," said Dad, "that might be a good idea. If it's not out of your way."

"No no, it is—EEP—in the same direction as Venus," said BZ.

　　穆迪與史凱莉坐進車裡，一直爭吵個不停。這也是我最後一次看到他們。有時候我很好奇，穆迪是否真的找到外星人存在的證據。

　　「我該回我的星球去了。」BZ說，「我可以——咿噗——順道載你們一程嗎？」

　　「既然我們只剩下十三分錢，」老爸說，「這是個好主意，如果你不用繞路的話。」

　　「不會、不會，這是——咿噗——和回金星相同的方向。」BZ說。

Chapter 9

On Monday I told the kids in school.

"There's no such things as UFO's," said Vernon Manteuffel. He doesn't know anything. Also, he sweats a lot.

"There may be intelligent life on other planets," said my best friend, Spencer. "But there's no evidence it has ever visited Earth."

The only person who believed me was Andrew Clancy, the kid who's always trying to top me.

"I think Zack's telling the truth," said Andrew.

第九章

　　星期一我跟同學說我遇到外星人的事。

　　「才沒有幽浮這回事。」馬富男說。他什麼都不懂，而且還超級會流汗。

　　「其他的星球上可能會有高等生物，」我最好的朋友史賓賽說，「但還沒有證據顯示他們曾經來過地球。」

　　唯一相信我的人是安德魯‧克蘭西，這個傢伙總是想要贏過我。

　　「我認為札克說的是真的。」安德魯說。

"You do?" said Spencer.

"Sure," said Andrew. "There *is* intelligent life on other planets. And space creatures *have* visited Earth. In fact, I was on board a UFO myself. And it was a whole lot bigger than the one Zack was on, I can tell you that."

OK, so no one really believed me. But they sure had trouble explaining where Dad and I got that 143 karat diamond!

「你相信他？」史賓賽說。

「當然，」安德魯說，「其他星球上是有高等動物，而且外星人曾經造訪過地球。事實上，我自己就搭過幽浮，它比札克搭的那艘還要大得多，我可以跟你們保證。」

好吧，沒有人真的相信我說的話，但他們肯定無法解釋，我和老爸得到的那顆一百四十三克拉的鑽石是從哪來的！

札克檔案08

到了金星請左轉

原著作者	丹‧葛林寶（Dan Greenburg）
譯　　者	陳家輝
出版公司	哈佛人出版有限公司（H. I. Publishers, Inc.）
執 行 長	張錦娥（Gina Chang）
文　　編	趙曉南（Nadia Chao）‧聞若婷（Michelle Wen）
	郭啓宏（Arthur Kuo）‧洪采薇（Therisa Hung）
地　　址	110 台北市信義區基隆路一段380號6樓
電　　話	02-2725-1823
傳　　真	02-2725-5962
Blog	http://tw.myblog.yahoo.com/harvard_inspired/
E-mail	harvard_inspired@yahoo.com.tw
會計稅務顧問	呂旭明會計師
總 代 理	農學股份有限公司
出版日期	西元2007年10月 初版
定　　價	新台幣199元

國家圖書館出版品預行編目資料

到了金星請左轉／丹‧葛林寶（Ｄａｎ
Greenburg）著；傑克‧戴維斯（Jack　E.
Davis）繪；陳家輝譯. --初版. -- 台北市：
哈佛人, 2007〔民96〕
面；　公分. --（札克檔案；8）
中英對照
譯自：Hang a Left at Venus
ISBN 978-986-7045-34-8 （平裝附光碟）

874.59　　　　　　　　96016512